Melody's Miracle

Book 3 in Clover Creek Community

Kirsten Osbourne

Copyright © 2023 by Kirsten Osbourne

Unlimited Dreams Publishing

All rights reserved.

Cover design by Erin Dameron Hill/ EDH Graphics

No part of this book may be reproduced in any form or by any electronic or mechanical means including information storage and retrieval systems, without permission in writing from the author. The only exception is by a reviewer, who may quote short excerpts in a review.

This book is a work of fiction. Names, characters, places, and incidents either are products of the author's imagination or are used fictitiously. Any resemblance to actual persons, living or dead, events, or locales is entirely coincidental.

Kirsten Osbourne

Visit my website at www.kirstenandmorganna.com

Chapter One

Melody's heart felt as if it were beating out of her chest. She was marrying a stranger. A stranger who had four grown children of his own. She had just turned forty, having been married since she was eighteen with no children at all.

Her husband had died just two months before. He had accidentally shot himself in the foot, and it had turned into gangrene, and he'd died while out hunting. He had loved her more than anyone had ever been loved, and she would miss him every day of her life. But the trail was just too hard for a woman traveling alone, and this little town seemed to understand.

Of course, calling Clover Creek a town was stretching the imagination just a bit. The town consisted of people who had set out on the trail over a year before, and they'd made it all the way to Oregon City and turned and come back. It was just one company, so the area was very sparsely populated.

By marrying this stranger beside her, she would ensure that she not only didn't have to continue on the trail, but she would also have a place to live and someone to provide for her. This was truly the only answer if she wanted to be done with the ridiculously long journey.

Jacob Appleby seemed a nice enough man for the fifteen minutes she'd talked with him before agreeing to marry him. Her dear husband, Gideon, had courted her for three years before her pa had agreed to let her marry him. He would be rolling over in his grave if he saw what she was doing now, but his daughter-in-law, Fiona, had spoken highly of him, and she would know.

Melody shook her head. She hadn't chosen an easy road, but she was determined to see it through.

The pastor cleared his throat. "Today, we are joining together two couples in holy matrimony. Mrs. Melody Nunc will marry Mr. Jacob Appleby first, and then Mrs. Doris Brown will marry Mr. Andrew Jefferson."

Everyone had gathered there, in the pews, waiting for the weddings to start. That was the way it was on the trail and in the newly growing west. Having found a place where she could call home, meant the world to Melody.

The pastor—she'd heard him called both Pastor Jed and Pastor Scott—continued quickly through the ceremony. When Jacob was told he could kiss her, he brushed a soft kiss across her cheek. She was thankful for that. Who wanted their first real kiss to be in front of an entire congregation full of people?

Jacob and Melody moved out of the way, so the pastor could repeat everything for Mr. Jefferson and Doris, who had become a good friend of Melody's on the trail. She wasn't certain why Doris was being called Mrs. Brown though. She'd never been married.

The rest of the evening passed in a blur. Melody felt like she was being treated like a queen as the townsfolk welcomed her and Doris. They all stopped their party by nine, so they could be up early for work the following day. It would be hard for Melody to see so many of her newfound friends head out on the trail again, but she was happy to not be going with them. Maybe her feet would stop aching so much.

After the small party, Jacob drove her to her wagon, and together, the two of them took what was needed. The wagon would sit there on the side of the trail until someone took it apart. There was no reason to keep it.

Instead, they took all the clothing from the wagon and what food was salvageable. They would add to Jacob's food stores. "I hope you enjoy cooking," Jacob said. "My daughter and daughters-in-law are downright tired of bringing me supper every night."

"I do enjoy cooking. Am I right that your youngest son will be living with us?"

"He shares my cabin with me right now. But my house should be built by the end of next week. He can stay in the cabin, and we'll take the house. He'll probably drop by for supper every night, though. He's a worse cook than I am."

Melody nodded. "I don't mind doing for both of you. Even after we move, he can bring his laundry for me to wash."

"I'll let him know. I'm certain he'll be pleased."

"I wish it wasn't so late in the season," Melody said. "I would like to be able to grow a kitchen garden for us."

Jacob shook his head. "Don't you start trying to garden this year. Between my two daughters-in-law, they have a garden big enough to feed half the town. I'm sure if you help them put up the vegetables, there will be no problem sharing."

"Your daughter didn't garden?"

Jacob laughed. "No, my Henri is in the family way, and bending is not something she's willing to do right now. She spent a lot of time helping the others after they married, so there's no reason for her to help this year. I'm sure she'll be helping after the baby is born."

Melody sighed. "I always expected to have children, and now here I am, having a grandchild. I never got to have children."

"I'm sorry," Jacob said. "I can't imagine life without my four."

"I'm barren." Melody spoke the words as if they were her secret shame.

"I'll just share my four with you. It'll all be good."

She smiled. "As long as you share that grandbaby with me, that's all I need." Pulling the last of her personal belongings from the back of the wagon, she put them into the back of her husband's wagon. "That's all. Hopefully if someone is in need of anything, they'll dig through the wagon and find what they're looking for."

"I'm sure they will. I know for our company on the trail, we shared everything."

"As have we. I found being a widow on the trail difficult, but people helped as much as they could. I made some very good friends after my husband died."

"How long ago was that?" he asked, staring straight ahead. He almost felt guilty that he was taking a bride home less than a year after he'd lost his sweet Nellie. But he needed to let his children and their spouses not be responsible for feeding him or doing his laundry. He knew it was a burden for Henri and his daughters-in-law.

"Two months," she responded. "My first inclination was to turn tail and head home, but I couldn't. A woman traveling alone would have become a victim of Indian attacks or wild animals. No, it wasn't a good idea to go back home, so I stayed with my company."

"What were you and your husband's plans once you made it to Oregon City?"

"My husband would have farmed, which he loved, and I hoped to open my very own millinery shop. I've always enjoyed the art of hat making."

He smiled a little. "If you still want to do that, I'll help you."

She shrugged. "I don't know if that's what I want anymore at all. It will be nice to have a big family. I always wanted children, but it just never happened for us. I'm sure I'm barren."

"Well, you will have children and grandchildren. My daughter is expecting her first. She's due in another month or so, I think. I honestly haven't paid a ton of attention to her when she's spoken about the babe. I look forward to being a grandfather, but the details of my daughter carrying a baby are things my wife would have loved, but I have no use for."

"When did you lose your wife?"

"End of September last year. We were on our way back here from Oregon City."

"She almost made it the whole way." It seemed sadder to Melody that his wife had died so close to their destination. "Cholera?"

"No. She just had a harder time every day. Clothes were just hanging off her. When she died, it was a blessing to her. But I'll never stop missing her, I don't suppose." Using the leads, he guided the team up the steep hill. "We live at the top of the hill. There's a beautiful view, and you can see the whole town."

"That sounds amazing," she said.

"Wait until you see it! Right now, I just have a small cabin that I share with my youngest son, Bastian, but our house is almost built. It won't be huge, but I don't think we'll need much. Bastian will stay in the cabin after we've moved out."

"Is Bastian short for Sebastian?" she asked. She didn't mind the idea of one of his adult children living with them, but she worried about the wedding night. It would be very awkward with his son in the cabin.

"Yup. I've got three boys and the youngest was a girl. Finally. I swear my wife would have insisted on twelve children if that's what it took to get a girl. Nellie named her Henrietta, and she was so sad when we all took to calling her pretty little girl Henri."

Melody smiled. "I think that would have bothered me as well. I used to dream about what I would name my little girls. Elizabeth was my favorite. Or Cassandra. There are so many nice nicknames for both. The child could practically name herself."

They reached the top of the hill and she could make out some cabins in the twilight. He turned left and stopped the wagon in front of a cabin that seemed larger than the others. He helped her down and invited her to investigate the cabin, while he unhitched the team and cared for the horses.

Melody opened the door, calling out Bastian's name. She didn't know if he'd been at the party, but she didn't want to frighten him if he didn't know his father had married.

Married. She looked down at her finger, which still bore Gideon's ring. It seemed strange that she was still wearing it and married to another man, but Jacob certainly hadn't taken a wedding ring to a party so he could marry a random stranger.

What a strange situation to be in.

She looked around the cabin, noting the fireplace was the only place to cook. She sighed. She wanted a real stove again. Cooking over a fire got old quickly.

There was no pump in the kitchen, so she knew she'd be toting water. She had no idea where the creek was, but she had to assume that's where water would be coming from. Hopefully one of his daughters-in-law would be willing to help her for a few days. Then she would know where everything was, and she could be on her own.

As she walked around, she could hear the hollowness beneath the wood floor, and she knew there was a cellar. She clapped her hands together. Hopefully Jacob had put a cellar in the new house as well, and she could store foods down there.

She was surprised to see a doorway, and when she opened the door, she found herself in a bedroom. The bed hadn't been made, but there was a dresser for clothes. This must be Jacob's room. They would have privacy after all.

Going back into the main room again, she saw there was a loft and immediately understood that was where Bastian would sleep. Oh, that made things so much easier.

The door opened and she turned to look, spotting a tall young man. He grinned at her. "Should I call you Ma?" he asked.

Melody laughed softly. "I think you can just call me Melody."

"All right. I sure hope you're a good cook. I'm looking forward to delicious meals. Night!" With that, Bastian climbed the ladder up into the loft.

Melody shook her head. The man had no manners whatsoever, which surprised her greatly. She would have thought a man like Jacob would have taught manners to all of his children.

Melody set about tidying up the bedroom while she waited for Jacob to come inside. The sheets looked like they could use a good wash, but she could do that the following day. Or perhaps she'd stay in the house barefoot all day so the blisters on her feet could heal.

By the time she'd swept the bedroom and straightened everything up, Jacob had come in carrying her belongings. He set her trunk at the foot of the bed. "You look tired."

"I've been keeping trail time," she said with a smile. "I'm always tired."

"You should take a couple of days to rest before you get too involved with the chores my daughters will get you caught up in. They have a huge garden, and I know they're planning to do a little harvesting tomorrow."

"I'll help if they need me." She sat down on the edge of the bed, and unlaced her shoes and took them off. They were her spare pair for the trail, and she'd only been wearing them for a week. When her socks came off, he stared at her feet.

"You need to rest more than a day or two. Your feet are bloody!"

"It's the new shoes. I didn't think to wear them for a little bit at a time, and I ended up with holes in my other pair. I've had to wear these for twenty miles per day for a week now, and they're broken in now, but they still rub the blisters." She wiggled her toes and sighed. "I'm so thankful I don't have to walk tomorrow." She pulled a clean pair of socks from her trunk. "No need to get the sheets all bloody."

He shook his head. "I'm not touching you tonight. I think we need a little time to get to know each other first."

"That would be very kind."

"You're injured anyway."

She smiled. "It could have been much worse."

"Yes, it could have," he said. "All right. I'm turning down the lamp. Do you mind changing with me in here if it's dark?"

Melody bit her lip, thinking about it. "I suppose not." She did mind, but they would need to get used to one another. They'd both been married, so they knew how marriage worked.

When the light was off, she changed into her nightgown and climbed under the covers. "It's surprisingly cold this evening," she said.

He climbed in beside her, and she said a silent prayer that he was wearing a nightshirt. "It's always cold at night. It's the altitude."

"I can't say I don't like it," she said with a smile.

"I like it too. I can't think of another place that I'd rather be."

Melody closed her eyes. "I hope you don't mind, but I have a feeling I'm going to fall straight to sleep."

"Sleep. And don't worry about getting up early to cook in the morning. Bastian and I can cook our own breakfast."

When he got no response, he realized she'd already fallen asleep. Remembering his time on the trail, he didn't blame her one bit. She'd need to be coddled for a little while, but then he'd have a wife again. Married life kept him happy.

Chapter Two

When Melody woke the following morning, it was well after sunup and Jacob was no longer in bed with her. She got up quickly, wincing as her feet hit the floor. The socks she'd put on the night before were covered in blood, but that was nothing new. She changed into her day dress, hoping there was enough laundry to make it worth her time. She truly needed some clean clothes.

After dressing, she went into the main room of the cabin to find Jacob and Bastian eating their breakfast. "I'm so sorry. I overslept. You should have woken me!"

Jacob shook his head. "No, I shouldn't have. I left a plate on the edge of the fireplace for you."

Melody grabbed a towel and carried the plate to the table with it. She knew how hot a plate could get from staying so close to the fire that way. Then she joined Jacob and Bastian at the table. Bowing her head, she said a quick prayer over her meal, thanking the Lord for a safe place to heal and the food he provided.

"Who cooked?" she asked, looking at the poorly cooked eggs and bacon on the plate in front of her.

"I did," Jacob said. He sounded so proud saying it that Melody knew it was his best effort.

Taking her first bite of the oversalted eggs, she carefully kept her face neutral so no one would know what she was thinking. "Thanks for cooking, Jacob, but wake me next time. It's my job to feed the two of you."

Jacob nodded. "I do think you should heal first."

"I'm doing my best to heal quickly, but I won't be shirking my duties as a wife."

"I appreciate that." Jacob knew he wouldn't be waking his wife for a good long while though. She'd just lost her husband, and her poor feet. He wanted to carry her everywhere.

After choking down as much breakfast as she could, Melody asked, "I assume I need to fetch stream water for the laundry?" She would wash all the sheets and make sure her clothes were all clean. Most of her things were filthy from the trail. They'd turned filthy as soon as they were clean. There was so much dust and mud on the trail, it was ridiculous.

Jacob gave her a look that told her what he thought of her jumping right into housework. "You don't need to do laundry yet. Let yourself rest for a day or two."

"All of my clothes are filthy from the trail. They need to be washed. I'll do the sheets and quilts as well. Do either of you have clothes that need to be washed?"

"I do," Bastian said. "And I'll fetch water, so you don't have to. Maybe the girls can come over today and help you get situated."

Jacob was disgusted with his son, but Bastian had never been good about understanding others. If it wasn't said straight out, he missed it. "I suppose I can't stop you."

"I'm glad you see things my way," Melody said with a smile.

Jacob shook his head. "I see that you're as stubborn as my first wife." He carried his plate over to the small worktable, and set it there. "I suppose you won't let me do the dishes either?"

Melody bit back a laugh. Her first husband had never allowed her to talk back to him that way. It seemed she would have a little more authority in this home than she had her last. "I'll handle the dishes, dear."

Jacob mumbled something under his breath that she couldn't quite hear, before he stormed out of the cabin.

Bastian looked at the closed door. "Pa must be working on the house today. Otherwise he would have waited for me."

Melody looked at Bastian for a moment and smiled. "I think he may have been mad at me."

"Why? He hates doing dishes, and you said you'd do them. That seems like he'd be happy to me."

Melody just grinned. She'd known people who didn't fully grasp other people's emotions. They were usually good people. "Maybe."

Bastian carried his plate to the worktable. "I'll go get your water now." On his way out the door, Bastian plopped his hat on his head, and she sat at the table shaking her head.

Melody already felt that her new home was very welcoming. She got up and carried her mostly untouched plate to the others. As soon as Bastian was back with the water, she'd do the dishes and then start laundry, her most loathsome chore.

She was surprised to hear a knock at the door, and hurried over. Fiona stood there with a smile on her face. "Hello. Your new husband came over and told me you were unwell. He said you'd need help with the housework today. Emma will be here soon as well, though Henri will only come if Roy drives her up the hill. She's too far along for all that climbing."

Melody sighed. Jacob had found a way around her stubbornness. She hadn't really wanted that, but what could she say? "Come in. Bastian is fetching water for me, and I plan to do laundry today."

Fiona looked down at Melody's socked feet and gasped. "Oh, Melody. You can't do laundry on those feet!"

"I don't have any other feet to do laundry on!"

"I know what we'll do. I hate mending. So I'll go and get my mending for you, and you can sit and work on that while Emma and I do your other chores for you. It'll be fun!"

Melody sighed. She'd have to remember that Jacob was tricky about those things. At least the way the other women were handling things, she'd feel like she was contributing.

Fiona hurried away just as Bastian returned with the water. Maybe she couldn't do laundry, but she could at least stand long enough to do dishes. She hung the water in a large cookpot on the hook over the fireplace to warm while she scraped what was left on the plates into a bowl. It could be fed to the chickens later. She knew there must be chickens because there were eggs.

It was going to be so nice to be settled and not wondering if there would be enough food to make it all the way to Oregon City. Her trip had been cut short, but into a much better situation than she'd imagined.

She had just finished putting the last dish away when Emma and Fiona returned with their mending.

Fiona put her hands on her hips. "Melody! You were supposed to leave that for us."

"I need to be able to do for my new family." Melody couldn't understand why the other women didn't understand that.

Emma smiled. "When I was first married, I couldn't cook worth anything. Jared was always bragging about what a wonderful cook Henri was, and I felt absolutely worthless. But I became a better cook under Henri's tutelage."

Fiona nodded. "And I felt badly that I was joining a family that already had so many women, and I wasn't able to feed my father the way I had. He's married now, so some of that guilt is dissipating, but I'm happy to be able to contribute. So today, we'll help you, while you help us with that dreadful mending. I don't know how many pairs of socks Sam has torn this summer alone. I fear you'll be busier than we are."

"I would think there would be mending here as well. I'll have to get on that!" Melody set down the towel she'd used to dry the dishes, and looked around, trying to figure out where men would hide a mending basket.

"We're doing your work, so you have to do ours," Fiona said quickly. She pointed to a rocking chair, where both she and Emma had set their mending down. "Now, please mend."

"I have to get the laundry for you!" Melody protested.

Emma shook her head. "I'll get the laundry."

Melody sighed, knowing she'd been beaten. There were two of them and only one of her. "I'd like all bedding washed today as well as my clothes from the trail. I can get those for you."

Fiona went to the bedroom and came out a short while later with not only all the bedding but also her clothes. "Before you say anything, we're going to fix lunch and supper today as well. If you want to argue about it, let's get it over with."

Melody couldn't help but laugh. "You two are as strong-willed as I am."

"We're proud of that fact too." Emma grinned at her as she climbed into the loft to get the laundry from there, tossing them onto the floor from upstairs and then climbing down. "I have no idea when the last time Bastian slept with sheets was. They were on the floor on the other side of the loft."

Fiona shook her head. "He needs to sleep between the sheets."

"You'd think..." Emma said.

"All right. Water is boiling, I think we'll go out and deal with the laundry. And you stay put!" Fiona said, glaring at Melody.

"I'm mending." Melody had already finished two socks, which she'd then matched and put back into the basket they came from. She didn't want to send the wrong mending back to either of the girls.

Emma stopped at the door, her arms full of dirty linens. "Do you want to move your chair out so you can talk to us while we do the wash?"

Melody nodded emphatically. "I would adore that. I was told you two have a kitchen garden..."

Fiona laughed. "It's become a bit more than a kitchen garden. We have a little of everything in there. It's been fun working on it with Emma." She dropped the wash onto the ground and went back into the cabin for the boiling water. "And don't worry. We made sure there would be enough for Pa and Bastian, and I think we all had in our heads we'd get him married off when the wagons started coming through. There's plenty to feed four families."

"Enough for when Bastian marries?" Melody asked.

"I'm hoping Bastian waits another year or two," Emma said. "He's not ready. I mean, he could provide for a family with no problem, but he's not good enough with words for a woman to be able to tolerate him for long. We'll teach him."

Melody smiled. "Perhaps I can work on teaching him in the evenings."

"The men don't come in until dark during the summer, and dark comes awfully late. There are plenty of times they take a break for supper, and head right back out. That's why the ranch is doing so well right now."

"I see. Well, then I'll teach him during the winter."

"He won't live with you in the winter," Emma reminded her. "He's going to stay in the cabin while you move into the big house."

Melody got her chair outside and situated herself with the mending. Looking up for the first time while it was light out, she saw the house. "Oh, that's a grand house!"

Fiona smiled. "And almost finished. Sam said another couple of weeks."

"I will be so fortunate to live there. You girls will help me clean it when it's done being built?"

"Of course we will!" Emma said.

"I'll feel like a queen living there." Melody could see the picture windows that were in. In fact, the outside of the house looked finished. Soon, she'd live there. She'd made a good choice when deciding to marry Jacob. Not only was he kind and thoughtful, but he was also providing her with a beautiful home.

They all chatted while Melody sewed and the girls did the laundry. Melody learned a lot about the other two, which was fun for her. "I wish Henri was here," Emma finally said. "She's missing out on getting to know you."

"I'll hitch up the team and go get her after we have lunch," Fiona said. "I don't mind."

Melody frowned. "Hitching a team is hard work." She'd had to spend a month hitching oxen to her wagon every morning and then driving all day instead of being with the other women. It had been the hardest month of her life. At least while Gideon had been alive, she hadn't had to do men's work as well as women's work. She got blisters from walking 20 miles a day. How did she do that while driving a team. Maybe she hitched it and some boy drove it

"I don't mind," Fiona said. "I sometimes go to visit my father alone, and I hitch and unhitch the wagon. I like to make sure he's well-fed and isn't living in filth."

"Then you should go!" Emma said with a smile. "I'll cook lunch for us all, and you go get her before lunch. Then she can eat with us, and we can all rejoice that there's a Henri in our lives."

Melody nodded. "I'd adore getting to know her. It seems as if everyone holds her in high regard."

"Oh, we do. She's annoyed that things she used to do easily are so hard now, though. I'll have her bring her mending so she can sit with you while we do whatever needs to be done," Fiona said.

"That sounds lovely. Having another invalid beside me while I work." Melody frowned. "Will the men be here for their lunch?"

Emma shook her head. "No, they tend to eat jerky for their noon meal, and then they come in starving around six. It's easier for them to just stay together and finish whatever it is they're doing."

Melody heard the distant sounds of a hammer. "I think they may be working on the house. I hear a hammer."

Emma shrugged. "They might be out repairing fences as well. One of Fiona's goats broke through a fence again last night, and it will need to be repaired today."

Melody smiled. "Goats? You have goats?"

Fiona nodded. "We have an entire menagerie of animals. Sam trains horses to sell. There are cattle, goats, kittens, horses, and chickens. There may be some I'm forgetting."

"We'll have a dog soon. My pa's dog is going to pup any day now. We'll take one to be a ranch dog," Emma said.

"Well, I certainly can't be lonely with all of those animals around, can I?" Melody asked.

"No, you can't," Fiona said. "The goats were my idea because I love goat cheese so much. We have four nannies and a billy. I'm hoping we can make cheese to sell or even sell off some of the offspring. I do love goats."

Melody grinned. "I wonder what kind of animal I should raise."

"The chickens are mine," Emma said. "My ma has always raised chickens, so they're a bit of a pet project for me. Besides, eggs are needed. And we are getting enough of a flock that I'll be able to start butchering some of the pullets."

"It sounds like all of you work together to keep this ranch going."

Fiona nodded. "And don't you let any of the menfolk tell you differently."

Chapter Three

Their lunch consisted of soup and day old bread, reminding Melody that she needed to bake some bread. "I think I'll bake some bread after lunch. I can't believe I didn't think to do that."

Henri looked under the table at Melody's bloody socks. "You'll sit with me, and Emma or Fiona will bake bread. They're both excellent cooks."

"I'm surprised you're not making gowns for the baby."

"I have a bunch at home. I thought I'd just mend today so we can complain about how hard men are on clothes while we work."

Emma laughed. "We're not going to let you stand to work today, Melody. Get used to the idea so we can stop arguing every ten minutes."

Melody sighed. "I just feel like I should be helping."

"You are helping. You're mending clothes," Fiona said.

So while Henri and Melody watched, Fiona and Emma did the lunch dishes and started a beef pot pie for supper. "I'm ready for fall," Henri said wistfully. "I love all the meat the men hunt and provide for us to put up and cook with all winter. Last year was a whirl because of how late in the year we arrived, but I'm certainly glad we did it as we did."

"And how was that?" Melody asked.

"Well, last autumn was just Emma and me. And her mother and sisters of course. We all worked together to put up the game the men brought us. Roy did the bulk of the hunting," Henri said proudly. "I'm thrilled with all he brought in, though we all shared everything."

Emma smiled. "Jared brought in a bear because no one in his family likes bear meat. We both love it, so we had it as a treat whenever we wanted."

"What did your mother do to help?" Melody asked Emma.

Emma laughed. "She mostly stayed out of the way. My mother is the worst cook this side of the Mississippi. Her specialty is jerky, and that's the only thing she cooks really well. The jerky the men have for lunch every day was made by her. Well, most of it. Henri's is a bit better of course, but no one will tell my Ma that."

Henri grinned. "I was happy she was so handy with jerky because my hands were full drying and canning all the other meat the men brought in." She nodded toward Emma. "And Emma was a huge help. Her sisters followed my instructions exactly."

"That was so much work!" Emma said, shaking her head. "But I'm glad we did it, and I'll gladly do it again every year for the rest of my life."

Henri laughed. "I'm hoping for light duty this year. There are more of us, and I should have a newborn by then. Although it feels like I've been expecting for three years."

Melody smiled. "I hope you'll allow me to be the grandmother of your baby. I'm barren, so I was never able to have babies of my own, and I so wanted them."

"Of course you'll be my baby's grandmother," Henri said with a smile. "He or she will have two grandmothers to spoil her."

"Thank you so much!"

"We'll all be providing you with grandchildren," Emma said. "I have a feeling there will be many."

"I do hope you're right!" Melody had always envisioned herself with a babe in her arms, and it had just never happened for her. Melody threw another pair of socks into one of the baskets. "I do believe your mending is done." She got to her feet. "Let me see if I can find any mending that Jacob or Bastian needs done unless you have something for me to do."

Emma sighed. "Let me go look for mending they need done. You are not climbing into that loft with your feet looking like they are."

Fiona walked over to Melody and got to her knees, carefully taking one of Melody's feet, putting it on her lap, and gently removing the sock. She looked at the mess of a foot in her hands, covered in blood and blisters. "I think we need to put something on it other than a sock. I have some bandages at my cabin if you don't want the doctor to take a look at them."

"I certainly don't need a doctor for blisters on my feet," Melody said. She couldn't believe her new family was making such a fuss over something that must have happened to them on the trail as well.

"I have an ointment my mother taught me to make. I'll fetch that and the bandages, and we'll get them cleaned up nicely." With that, Fiona stood and put some of the water that was left on the fireplace to heat. Then she hurried out the door.

"I wish people wouldn't make such a fuss over me," Melody said.

"I completely understand the feeling," Henri responded patting her huge middle.

Emma returned with more mending for Fiona to do, moving both of the baskets she'd finished out of the way. "One more basket of mending. I don't know how we'll keep you busy tomorrow though."

"Hopefully my feet will be better tomorrow."

Emma frowned. "I don't think that's at all in the realm of possibility."

Melody sighed. "Probably not, but I would adore being able to explore the area."

Fiona rushed back inside with a basket with bandages and a small jar. "What's in the ointment?" Melody asked, not sure if she wanted whatever the other woman was holding slathered on her feet.

"Don't worry about it. My ma used to tell me it would heal anything from burns, to cuts, to bug bites. It'll help." Fiona set the basket on the table and carried the pot over to Melody. "The water is hot but shouldn't be too hot. Let's soak your feet in it, and when they're thoroughly clean, I'll put the ointment and bandages on them. I don't want you to wear socks over the bandages."

Melody nodded. "I won't."

Thirty minutes later, Melody's feet felt much better than they had. "I'm going to be able to do more tomorrow," she said. "Your ointment is magical."

Fiona shook her head. "No, but it will help. Now Emma and I are going to get the clothes off the line while you and Henri get some more sewing done."

"They are very bossy," Melody said to Henri once they were outside.

"They've treated me the same all summer. I didn't even get to help with the garden, and though I know I'd have been in the way, it would have been nice to feel useful."

Melody nodded. "I agree. I do not feel useful right now."

"Oh, you should. Both of them hate mending more than anything. I've listened to them complain about it. You really did help them." Henri smiled at her sisters who were laughing over something as they took sheets off the line. "They both prefer to be on their feet and busy all the time."

"As do I," Melody said. "Well, before the trail I was that way. Not sure I'll ever willingly walk twenty miles in a day again."

"I don't think any of us will!" Henri shook her head. "Mrs. Mitchell, our local midwife, told us every day that it was a death march. So many people died that it really did feel like a death march."

"It was the same with our company," Melody said. "My Gideon wasn't the first to die, and he certainly wasn't the last. I'll miss him every day for the rest of my life."

Henri reached over and covered her stepmother's hand with her own. "I lost my mother between Oregon City and here. I don't think I've ever known such grief. If it had been my Roy, I'm not sure I ever would have gotten over it. How can you lose the person you chose to spend your life with and ever stop grieving?"

"I'm sorry for your loss," Melody said. "I lost my mother when I was young, and my father sent us off to live with her sisters. For almost a year, he couldn't bear to look at us, and finally, he took us home again. Nothing was ever the same though."

"How old were you?" Henri asked.

"Just six. I can't even remember what she looked like."

"I'm so sorry. I grieve for my mother, but she taught me so much. I had her until shortly before I married. I cannot imagine what my life would have been like without her."

Melody smiled. "And I don't remember life with my mother. My father remarried when I was ten, and she was a kind woman. Thankfully, she took the time to teach me the womanly arts so that I could take care of Gideon like a good wife. She and I wept together when it was time for us to head west."

"She sounds like a wonderful stepmother. I'm sure you will be as well." Henri smiled at the older woman, feeling something for her she hadn't expected. She couldn't say she loved her just yet, but sitting and talking to her made her more inclined to love. She was a good woman.

The other two came back inside, first going up into the loft to straighten the mess Bastian had made out of it and make his bed for him, and then came down to do the same in the room Melody shared with Jacob. All of this love was spreading over her, and Melody found herself weepy. It wasn't often that people came into her life and treated her as if she was special.

Emma made a stew for supper as well as some rice to eat it over while Fiona made bread. "The bread will need to be removed from the fire," Fiona said. "But that should be possible for you. I need to get home and make supper for Sam."

Melody slowly got to her feet, carefully stepping, though the pain wasn't nearly as bad as it had been earlier. "Thank you for all you did for me today. I hope you'll let me labor in your garden as soon as my feet are healed."

Fiona smiled. "Of course! And I'll bring Sam over for breakfast in the morning so you don't have to eat what Jacob or Bastian cook. They are both terrible in the kitchen, and sometimes I think they try to cook the worst meal they can so the other will take over for them."

Melody laughed. "That explains the shells in the eggs I was given this morning."

Emma made a face. "My ma always got shells in the eggs. I'm so happy I don't have to eat her cooking any longer. I'll be here after breakfast, and then I'll make breakfast for you the following day, bringing Jared along with me."

"I'm not going to be an invalid forever!" Melody said, frowning. Even on the trail when she'd still had to do so much every day, no one had been trying so hard to help her.

Fiona laughed. "We know. You have our help until your feet heal, and we won't let you quibble about it." She looked at Henri. "Are you ready to go home?"

Henri nodded. "I need to put supper on the table for Roy."

"Of course you do. Have either the doctor or Mrs. Mitchell given you any idea when that baby is coming?"

"Mrs. Mitchell said another couple of weeks. The baby hasn't dropped yet, though I'm not terribly certain what that means."

"You have a doctor and a midwife here?" Melody asked. "What a blessing. We had many babies born on the trail, and somehow I became the midwife, but I had no idea what I was doing."

"There were many for us as well, but Mrs. Mitchell and Dr. Bentley were there to help. We lost a couple of babes along the way, but far fewer than we would have without the two of them." Fiona opened the door waiting for Henri to precede her.

"Every time someone mentions that infants die, I think I die a little inside," Henri said softly.

"Then it will never be mentioned in your presence again," Emma said. "I can't wait to be an aunt."

"I can't wait to be a grandmother!" Melody called after them as she closed the door. What a wonderful family she'd married into.

She removed the bread from the fire. It was just like the bread she'd made on the trail. More of a flat bread in a skillet. Not her favorite, but it would work.

Supper was ready and on the edge of the fire to stay warm. Melody looked around her and realized there wasn't much left to do. She worried it was wrong, but she was so tired, she climbed between the fresh, clean sheets and laid down for a nap. Surely Jacob would be pleased that she was resting as he'd instructed.

Not that he should get used to her doing as instructed. She'd never been particularly good at that, and she didn't think she ever would be.

As she closed her eyes, she stretched a little. She still missed Gideon with every fiber of her being, but being in a place where she was safe and she wasn't driving or walking...well, it was a dream come true. Now if only she could be certain her marriage would be the same.

Chapter Four

When Jared and Bastian arrived home, Melody was fast asleep. Rather than wake her, Jacob closed the door as quietly as he could.

Bastian frowned. "Why's she sleeping?"

"She's healing," Jacob said. "She's been on the trail for a long time. Remember how tiring that was?"

Bastian shrugged. "Guess it was."

"And her feet have blisters all over them."

"But she was going to cook for us!"

Jacob sighed. "Sniff deeply. You should be able to smell our supper."

Bastian walked over to the work table. "There's bread. And stew. And rice. We won't starve."

The door to the bedroom opened. "I'm sorry. I meant to rest my eyes for twenty minutes, and the next thing I knew, I could hear you. Let me set the table for supper."

Jacob looked at the bandages on her feet. "Bastian will do it. He doesn't want you hurting yourself any more than I do."

Bastian sighed. "I thought things were changing when you married. I guess it's the same as always around here."

Jacob glanced at Melody to see she was more amused than anything. "I'll be able to do everything once my feet heal," she said. "It won't be for long, Bastian."

Bastian sighed and set the table. He obviously thought she was just being lazy, but Melody could deal with that. She took a seat at the table perpendicular to where Jacob sat. Bastian simply set the table without a word, obviously annoyed it was his job still.

Once they were all seated, Jacob said a quick prayer. The stew was remarkably good. "This is delicious," Melody said to the others.

"Who made it? Do you know?" Jacob asked.

"Emma made it and Fiona made the bread. Henri and I worked on mending all day, so I didn't feel slothful. I just wish I could have helped with other things."

Jacob nodded. "I understand that. I'm glad the girls did as I instructed and made you sit as much as you could. Who bandaged you?"

"Fiona. She had some ointment her mother made, and some bandages. It's much better than wearing thick socks that stick to the wounds."

Bastian frowned at Melody. "Why'd you go and hurt yourself?"

"I wore out my first pair of shoes a couple of weeks ago, and I had to switch to new ones. The new ones blistered my feet badly because they weren't broken in. I have bleeding blisters all over them. As soon as they heal, I'll be able to do a lot more around the house. What Fiona put on them has really helped. I hope to be able to do my share within the next couple of days."

Jacob narrowed his eyes at that. "I don't know how smart that is," he said.

"I'm not going to laze about doing nothing. I've worked since I was a small child, and I'll work until the day they put me in the ground." She took a sip of the milk Bastian had served for them. "Thank you for setting the table, Bastian. I know you didn't want to."

"You'll do it soon?" he asked.

"I will do it soon." Melody enjoyed the meal immensely. Today had been the first decent meals she'd eaten but hadn't cooked since leaving for the trail. It was nice to be pampered a little, though she did wish she could do more.

After supper, she made her way to the basin and washed the dishes. She wasn't going to have trouble with Bastian simply because she was injured.

After supper, she went back to the rocking chair she'd spent most of the day in after retrieving her yarn and knitting needles. She thought it would be nice to make a little hat and booties for the grandbaby she was claiming as her own.

Jacob sat with a knife and a block of wood, whittling away at something. "What are you making?" she asked.

"I don't know yet. The wood will tell me."

She looked around the cabin and didn't see any other objects carved from wood. Surely Jacob had carved something before. "What do you usually make?"

"My wife enjoyed woodland animals, so I made an entire forest full for her. There's no room to put them out here, but we'll do that at the new house." Jacob paused turning the wood in his hands. "I cannot figure out what this wants to be."

"Something for the baby perhaps?" Melody suggested. She looked around and realized Bastian had disappeared.

"Today was a long day for the boy," Jacob told her, guessing at her thoughts. "He doesn't like change much, and having you here makes things hard for a little while."

"Do you know why?"

Jacob shook his head. "No, just always been that way. He's a good kid, always making jokes and teasing his siblings, but they're not here now. He does better when they're close. I've seen big changes in him in the last year, particularly since he moved out of Sam's cabin and back here."

"Sounds like he needs a wife."

"Eventually," Jacob agreed.

They sat in silence for a while, just working on their own projects. Thankfully it wasn't an uncomfortable silence, and Melody didn't feel the need to try to get Jacob to talk to her about anything. No, she understood that he'd already been married to the love of his life. She was just a poor substitute.

BY THE FOLLOWING MORNING, her feet were feeling much better, which was good, because it was Sunday, and that meant she'd meet new people at the church in town. Melody felt it was very strange to be just dropped into a community she knew nothing about, but as long as she did what she was supposed to do, she was sure all would be good.

Before making breakfast, she dug in her trunk for her hoop that went with her fullest dress for the church service, thinking she could go with her feet in bandages and not in shoes. If her skirt was full enough, no one would even notice.

She didn't know if other women would be in hoops or not, but it would allow her to go to church barefoot, something she needed.

It wasn't a simple task to cook breakfast while wearing a hoop skirt, but she managed. When the men woke, she had a delicious breakfast of pancakes and bacon waiting for them.

Bastian seemed pleased that she'd cooked breakfast, but still a little sullen. "What's on your mind, Bastian?"

Bastian shrugged. "I miss my brothers and sister. Pa, can we make your house bigger so we can all live together again?"

"No," Jacob answered. "Remember how much you liked living with just Sam? Soon you'll be able to live all by yourself. It will be good to spend some more time reading your Bible and reflecting on what you read."

Bastian nodded. "I can spend more time with the animals. Can the pup live with me?"

Melody remembered the mention of a puppy from the day before. "Do you think you'd like to take care of a dog?"

"Oh, yes. I already help with the cows, and the goats, and the chickens. I'm really good with animals."

Melody smiled. "I'm sure you are. You'll have to introduce me to all the animals once my feet are healed."

"I'd like that," Bastian said.

"I don't think even I've met all the animals," Jacob said. "Mind if I tag along on your tour?"

Bastian shook his head. "No, Pa. She asked me, and I'll teach her everything she needs to know."

Melody hid a smile by bowing her head. "So what does a rancher do in the winter?"

"Makes sure the cattle stay alive," Bastian said. "It's hard, because they want to be out and wandering around, but there's not enough for them to eat. But we don't have enough room for all of them to be in the barn. We did last winter though. So we'll keep all of the ones who are calving inside, and the others can go in and out. I like springtime the best. Roundup is so much fun, and we get to castrate most of the young bulls. That's fun too."

"And where do you take them to market?" Melody asked.

"We're not doing that yet this year," Jacob said. "We're building up our herd. We'll butcher the steers we have for our own food and to sell to others, but we need to keep every single cow."

Melody nodded. "That makes perfect sense to me. Will others in town need the food?"

"Oh, yes," Jacob said. "We have a boarding house in town that serves three meals per day, and now we have a store. I think the store will buy more than anyone else from us." He shrugged. "We aren't really planning on making much income this year."

"That won't hurt you?"

Jacob shook his head. "No, when we sold what we had back east, we planned to support ourselves on that money for two and a half years. We're going to be just fine."

"And all of your sons work with you? Henri's husband as well?"

"No, not Roy. He works with his own father, which is why she has a cabin on the hill, but not as high up as ours. On this level of the hill is only our family."

Melody nodded. "I see. But food is shared between the families?"

"Since Henri and Jared married siblings, we just share with all. Easier this way, and everyone benefits. That garden the girls have been working on is truly something to be proud of. I do hope they'll allow you to help them with it when it's time for harvest."

"I hope so too. I know they plan on sharing with us, but I want to be able to help with all of it. I've always enjoyed canning and drying meat. You'd think after the trail, I'd be tired of it, but I'm not."

"Good. You'll be a big help to them then. And once Henri's babe comes, she'll need time to rest after the birth."

Melody nodded. "I know. I am excited to be able to help her."

"That's a really fancy dress for church," Bastian said out of the blue.

"With this dress, I can wear bandages on my feet and not shoes. Thank heavens hoop skirts are still popular. Makes it easy for me to hide my injury."

Jacob shook his head. "I don't want you walking around though. If you go right in and sit in a pew and let people come to you, then you won't injure yourself more."

"I suppose I can do that." She didn't like the idea of sitting meekly waiting for people to come to her, but she wasn't going to heal if she was constantly on her feet. No, what Jacob said was definitely for the best.

"Good. I worry they'll become infected. Maybe we should have the doc look at them after church."

"Oh, no, they feel much better today. There's no need to bother the man."

Jacob nodded. "If they're still bothering you tomorrow, I'll have Fiona drive you."

Melody nodded. "I just don't want to put anyone out when I know they will heal on their own."

"We're going to play it safe," Jacob said. She could tell by the look on his face, he meant it, so she didn't bother to argue with him.

While the men did chores that morning, she finished the dishes, and decided to make the leftover stew for lunch. It would taste just as good the second time, and would be much easier to do than starting something from scratch. She really was trying to stay off her feet.

By the time everyone had finished their chores, it was time for church. Melody knew the dress she wore was too fancy for church, but she couldn't let herself care. Instead, she removed her apron and donned a hat that matched, ready to meet the new community she'd joined.

She marveled at the fact that an entire company had decided to settle in one place so they would be neighbors after the long walk across the west. She had learned that only two families hadn't joined the rest. The Blue family and the Cauldron family. The first had gone on to Seattle and the latter went east a ways.

Bastian came into the house after helping hitch up the wagon and said they were ready for her. She really hated getting her bandages dirty by walking across the ground, but she couldn't see a way around it.

Her steps were short and she studied everything on the ground before she stepped there, making sure she didn't injure herself worse.

When she finally reached the wagon, Bastian picked her up by the waist and set her on the seat. He obviously didn't want to wait for her to climb up on her own.

"Ready?" Jacob asked before removing the brake and starting down the hill.

"Yes," Melody responded.

Bastian was in the back and seemed comfortable there. She was glad, because she felt bad for taking what must have been his spot in the wagon.

"Would you like to go for a drive this afternoon?" Jacob asked. "I'd invite you for a walk, but I don't want you hurting your feet more."

"Neither do I. I'd rather be able to work and pull my own weight."

"I thought maybe we could have supper at the boarding house tonight. Margaret Prewitt is one of the finest cooks around. I don't think she's better than my Henri, but she's close."

"Then I look forward to eating both of their cooking." Melody liked how close-knit this community felt. She hadn't lived in such a welcoming place back east.

At the church, Jacob caught her waist and lowered her to her feet, watching the ground where he was setting her. When he offered his arm, she took it willingly, going into the church with him.

She'd been there for the party the night she'd met him, but it was different now. There was no lively music, and the smells of a feast didn't permeate the air. Jacob stopped at the first pew and she quickly sat down, arranging her skirt so her feet would be covered.

Emma and Henri made a beeline for her, while Jacob walked to a group of men at the back of the church. "You look beautiful," Emma said. "Brilliant way to hide your feet!"

Melody laughed softly. "I did what I could. I certainly didn't want to miss church on the first Sunday I was here."

"This church is the cornerstone of our community. During fall and winter, we have a quilting circle that meets on Wednesday afternoons. This doubles as the schoolhouse now that school has started for the year." Henri did her best to fill Melody in on the importance of the building. "We have socials here all spring and summer, where we all bring something and eat outside, then we dance. In the fall and winter, we have dances a couple of times a month here. All the men in town helped build it, so we all feel as if it's our very own. Pastor Jed and his wife Hannah live here with their baby. This church is the most important building in our entire community."

"I see that." Melody liked the idea of having a place to gather during the colder months. She'd heard stories of women hating being cooped up during winter so badly, they slowly went insane.

Emma looked at someone standing on the other side of Melody, so Melody turned. "Hannah, this is my new mother-in-law, Melody Appleby. Melody, Hannah Scott, the pastor's wife."

Suddenly, Melody understood why the pastor was called two different things. It made sense. "It's so good to meet you."

Hannah shifted the baby to her other hip. "I'm glad you joined our little community. I hope we've all made you feel welcome."

Melody smiled, assuring the younger woman she felt very at home, but her eyes were on the baby. She knew she'd never have one, but oh, how she longed for one.

Chapter Five

After church, where Melody met more people than she'd ever be able to remember, they went home and she reheated the leftover stew. After lunch, Jacob said, "If you feel up to it, I'll drive you out to Bear Lake. It's beautiful. Many swim and fish there. I've only been once, and that was to take Henri shortly after we arrived here. I shouldn't have taken a day off to take my daughter to see the lake, but I felt like she needed some time after her mother died, and before she married."

"How long were you here when she married?" Melody asked.

"Oh, a week or two. They didn't waste any time. And Jared and Emma were married a week later." Jacob took another bite of the stew. "I just need to marry this one off now," he said, nodding toward Bastian, his youngest son.

Bastian shook his head. "I'll marry myself off when I'm ready."

"When do you think you'll be ready?" Jacob asked.

Bastian shrugged. "When I meet the most beautiful girl in the world and decide she's the one I should marry."

"Did you look for that beautiful girl while the wagon train was in town?"

Bastian shook his head. "No. There wasn't anyone pretty enough."

Jacob grinned at Melody, not saying a word. He knew his wife understood Bastian in a way most women didn't. "Well, hopefully the next wagon train will have the girl you're looking for." Really, though, he hoped it wouldn't happen for a couple of years. There was no doubt in his mind Bastian would make a good husband, but he just wasn't ready yet. "So do you want to go for that drive?"

"Are you sure you can take time off work?"

"We try to follow the Sabbath around here. We couldn't at first because there was too much to be done, but now that we've gotten the initial construction out of the way, we can worship the Lord as we should."

Melody nodded. She was happy she hadn't been there for the initial rush of getting ready for winter. "It sounds like you had a tough winter here."

Jacob nodded. "We expected it though. Lots of work, but this year, even though there's still a great deal of work, we all feel like we're settled enough that this winter should be easier. Last winter there was no time to grow anything. This year we'll have most of the construction out of the way by the end of the month, and then we can hunt for the winter."

"I like to hunt," Bastian said.

"I like to fish," Melody whispered, pretending it was a huge secret.

"We'll go fishing together at the creek soon." Jacob was surprised that his wife enjoyed fishing, but it was another means to get food on the table.

"I'd like that." She frowned down at herself. "I'll put on a day dress before we go."

"You were the prettiest woman in the church," Jacob said, feeling out of place saying it. He was torn between being loyal to his late wife and being a good husband to the new one.

"Thank you," Melody said. It felt strange to get a compliment like that from a man other than Gideon, but Jacob was her husband now, and she would have to get used to him.

As soon as they'd finished their lunch, Melody washed the dishes and then changed into a simple day dress. When she walked back into the main room, Fiona was there with her basket of bandages and ointment. "We were just about to go for a drive."

Fiona nodded. "I just want to change your bandages and check on your feet. I'll check them daily for the next couple of days. We want to make sure they don't get infected."

"Do you mind waiting?" Melody asked Jacob.

"Not at all." Jacob sat down in the other rocking chair and started working on his whittling. He still didn't know for sure what he was making, but it didn't matter too much. He could burn that piece and start another if that's what he decided to do.

Fiona exclaimed over how well the blisters were healing. "I would think they would look much worse than this today. I think soaking them yesterday really helped."

Melody nodded, peering down at her feet. "They feel so much better."

"Good. We'll keep doing what we did to them yesterday until they're fully healed. Henri and Emma and I will all come over in the morning to help you with your chores. We do like to spend most days together."

"I'd like that a lot. But you have to know, as soon as I feel better, I'm coming over and helping you with something."

Fiona laughed. "That's fine. I want to make a rug for the front door, so Sam has a place to wipe his feet when he comes in."

"I could help with that." Melody was thrilled that the younger women were welcoming her into their world so easily.

After tying off the bandages, Fiona got to her feet. "We'll soak them again tomorrow," she said to Melody before disappearing out the door.

"It was sweet of her to come and fuss over my feet today." Melody was sick of the fussing, but she wasn't about to tell Jacob that.

Instead of letting her walk out to the wagon, Jacob swung her up in his arms and carried her, putting her onto the seat. "I guess I should be taking a courting buggy, but the wagon feels a lot more natural to me."

"I can understand that," she said. "I feel more comfortable in a wagon anyway."

"Good. You'll make a good rancher's wife then."

"I hope so. And, before I forget to say it, thank you for marrying me and making it so I don't have to keep traveling."

"No need to thank me. I'm just glad to have someone to make meals and clean the house." He glanced over at her as he turned at the church and headed through town. He hoped she would be ready to make love soon. He hadn't forgotten his wife, but this woman really was beautiful and a man had needs that didn't necessarily have anything to do with love.

As they drove, he told her about different people in the town. The girls had filled her in on many people, but his descriptions of them were so different from the others. He seemed to be able to paint a picture of a person that allowed her to see them in her mind. It was wonderful.

As soon as they could see the lake, he stopped driving, looking out over it. "I could go closer, but we probably should head back to town now. It's getting dark earlier."

"Yes, of course. That's fine with me. The lake is beautiful. Promise me we'll go and fish someday soon. Maybe on a lazy Sunday when we are observing the Sabbath."

"Fishing isn't work?" he asked.

"Not the way I do it." She gave him a sly grin that had him wondering about her.

"All right. Pack a picnic next Sunday, and we'll go right after church."

"Really?" she asked, clapping her hands together. She loved the idea of sitting on the shore with him, whether they fished or not. He was truly a good man.

They sat for a moment looking out at the lake, when Jacob surprised her by turning to her. "May I kiss you?"

Melody took a deep breath. She'd known this was coming, though she'd hoped it would wait until later. "You're my husband," she said softly in response.

"Is that the only reason you're willing to let me kiss you?" he asked.

She thought for a moment about the question. It was certainly most of the reason, but part of her had to wonder what his kisses would be like. Gideon had treated the marriage act as something to be done in a hurry, so she was unsure how other men did things. "No, it's not," she finally answered.

"Good," he said, leaning toward her and brushing his lips against hers. Instead of being quick about it, he took his time, toying with her lips with his own.

After a short while, he pulled away from her, a lopsided smile on his face. "I'd like to do that more often, if you'd be amenable."

Melody was surprised at the tingling in her lips and the quickening of her belly. Never before had she experienced such a thing from a mere kiss. "Yes, of course," she said, still thinking about how his lips had felt against hers. They'd slept together in a bed for two nights, and neither had made a move to be closer to the other. She had a feeling that was all about to change.

As they drove back, he kept the conversation light as he asked her questions about where she'd come from and what her family had been like before she'd married.

"Did you want children?" he asked, and tears sprang into her eyes.

"Yes, I always wanted half a dozen." She shook her head. "It wasn't meant to be."

"I suppose not. I'll share my children and grandchildren with you though."

"That's the kindest thing anyone has ever said to me," Melody replied, looking away from him for fear he'd see the tears drifting down her cheeks.

He reached over and took her hand in his. "I hope you'll be happy with me and my family." He couldn't believe how much he already cared for this woman. She seemed like a wounded bird to him, and he was desperate to help her fly again. Jacob was convinced he could do it, if given a little time. Then he smiled. They had the rest of their lives.

They stopped at the boarding house for their supper, and she met Margaret Prewitt. Margaret had a baby strapped to the front of her.

"Well, hello, Mrs. Appleby. I was hoping for a chance to speak with you at church this morning, but the baby was colicky, so I spent the entire service walking outside with him."

"It's very nice to meet you," Melody said. "What a beautiful baby."

"God has blessed me with three beautiful children. I never dreamed a boy would be so much different than his sisters even at such a young age." Margaret shook her head. "Listen to me babbling on. Would you like coffee, tea or water?"

Melody was a little afraid to drink water that she hadn't personally watched boil. "I'd love some tea."

"Mr. Appleby?"

"Coffee please."

A short while later, Mrs. Prewitt returned with their drinks and a moment later, plates filled with food. They didn't have a choice of meals, but what was served smelled absolutely delicious to Melody.

As soon as she took her first bite, her eyes widened. "This is delicious."

He smiled. "Mrs. Prewitt does a wonderful chicken and dumplings. I think they're even better than Henri's."

"I've heard lots of bragging about Henri's cooking. Is she really that good?"

"I believe with everything inside me that my first wife was the best cook in the world. And Henri is a better cook than her mother was. They loved to cook together. But neither ever liked to sew."

"I prefer to sew than cook, but I enjoy both." She took another bite of her food. "Would Mrs. Prewitt be offended if I asked for her receipt?"

"Not at all," Mrs. Prewitt said from behind her. "I'll write it out for you and give it to you before you leave. I'd bake cookies for you and take them to your house, but as you can see, I'm busy here."

"I can see that. I'd be happy to help out so you can sit a spell someday. Just let me know."

Mrs. Prewitt smiled. "Thank you. I may just take you up on that."

By the time they left the boarding house, Melody was uncomfortably full and carried the receipt for the delicious meal in her hands. "Thank you for taking me there."

Jacob shook his head. "I'm just thankful I had a way to keep you off your feet."

Melody wrinkled her nose. "I like to do for others. I always have."

"Do from a chair. Your feet look much better than they did that first night, but I'd like to see them completely healed, and that's not going to happen if you keep standing on them."

"You realize I have nothing but feet to stand on, right?"

"I'm not going to argue about it."

When they got home, he carried her inside before going back out to unhitch the team. Bastian came in a short while later, a big grin on his face. "Where were you?" she asked, happy to see him smiling.

"I had supper with Emma and Jared. Emma made a chicken pot pie, and it was delicious." Bastian looked at Melody skeptically. "Do you know how to make pot pie?"

"I certainly do. I'll make one for you and your pa soon."

"Am I going to eat with you after you move to the big house?"

"If you want to! I will always set a place at the table for you."

"Good. I don't much like to cook."

"Of course, you don't," Melody said. "You like doing men's work."

"I do." Bastian wandered toward his loft. "I'm turning in early."

As she watched him go, Melody couldn't help but smile. Bastian seemed a little odd, but he'd been much more relaxed that evening. It had done him some good to spend time with his brother and sister-in-law.

It wasn't much past dark, but Melody was already exhausted. She went into the bedroom and changed into her nightgown.

Jacob joined her a short while later. Seeing her in bed, he turned down the lamp before he undressed and put his nightshirt on. He'd promised himself he wouldn't make love to her until her feet were better, but that didn't mean he couldn't get her used to his touch. He'd wanted nothing more than to kiss her since their first kiss overlooking the lake.

Melody had made quite an impression on him, and he didn't think she even realized it.

Climbing into bed beside her, he reached toward her and kissed her. "You're a good wife, Melody Appleby."

Her hand went to the back of his neck and stroked the hair there. "That's because you're a good husband."

Chapter Six

The next morning, Melody felt like she was glowing. Every time she caught sight of Jacob, she thought about how he'd kissed her and touched her the night before. None of his touches had truly been intimate, but they felt as if they had been all the same.

As she made breakfast, she realized that her feet were now hurting very little. She was almost certain Fiona would let her skip the ointment and bandages.

As the men came in from their chores, Melody put breakfast on the table. "Good morning," she called pleasantly.

To her surprise, Jacob walked to her and kissed her very casually, as if it was something he did every morning. It didn't seem to phase Bastian even a little, so she continued with what she was doing.

After breakfast, she washed the dishes as the men headed to work. It wasn't long before she heard the sound of a wagon. Fiona, Henri, and Emma jumped down and hurried into the cabin. "What's our big project today?" Emma asked.

"I want to get the floors and walls scrubbed. This house needs a good fall cleaning before Jacob and I move to the big house."

"Have you seen inside yet?" Henri asked.

"I haven't. Have you?"

Henri nodded. "I helped Pa design the house, and I made sure I had him put in a kitchen any woman would be proud of."

"Is it close to ready?" Melody asked.

Emma nodded. "But we're not supposed to tell you."

"How close?" Melody asked.

"Before the week is out," Fiona said, sounding as excited about the whole thing as Melody felt.

"I know he said there would be a real stove. I'm very excited about that."

All three girls nodded. "I'll get started on sweeping," Fiona said. "You sit with Henri." She nodded to Melody as she said the last words.

"I don't think I need to. My feet are so much better this morning."

"Sit for one more day. I brought a book for you to read to all of us today." Fiona handed Melody a book.

When Melody glanced at it, she was surprised. It wasn't the Bible as she'd suspected it would be. The book was titled *Wuthering Heights*.

"This is what you want me to read?" Melody asked, looking at it warily. She'd been taught from a young age that reading anything but news or the Bible were not good for women.

Henri nodded as she worked on the tiny gown in her hands. "I want to hear it!"

"Where did this book come from?" Melody asked.

Emma laughed. "It's my mother's. She told me we should all read it together."

"Why haven't I met your mother yet, Emma? She seems like a very interesting person."

"Oh, she is. If you want to have a meal with her, make sure to invite her here though. I didn't know what good cooking was until after I married." Emma shook her head as she swept the floor.

Fiona boiled some water to use to scrub the floors. While the others worked on her home, Melody opened the book and began to read. Immediately, she was sucked into the story, and she could see what was happening in her imagination.

Frequently, when she looked up, the girls had paused in their work to just listen to the story. She read the first two chapters before she realized how much time had gone by. "We should have some lunch," Melody said.

The girls all looked at one another and laughed. "I think we all forgot we were supposed to be working," Emma said. "Let me throw some lunch together, and then we can listen to more after lunch."

Fiona frowned. "While you make lunch, I'm going to run home and get bandages and ointment."

"Look at my feet first," Melody suggested. "I don't think I need it anymore."

Fiona dropped to her knees in front of Melody and carefully unwrapped one of the bandages. She gasped. "Oh, you're right, Melody. They look amazing!"

"That's what I tried to tell you. They barely hurt."

Fiona bit her lip. "One more day of sitting, and we'll let you work tomorrow. Henri can read to us while we work. I don't think we're being idle because we are working while we listen."

Melody laughed. "Every time I looked up no one was working because they were all too enthralled by the story."

"We work hard," Emma said. "We should all get to read a book now and again."

Melody didn't argue. There was no point. The girls would do what they wanted to do anyway.

When Jacob got home that night, he found his wife setting the table for supper and putting the meal on. "You're not supposed to be on your feet so much!" Jacob protested.

"Even Fiona said my feet look much better. They only had me sit all day so I could read them a story."

He chuckled. "That sounds about right." He walked close to her and kissed her cheek. "You're really all right?"

"I really am. I promise."

Bastian came in late for supper, looking worried. "I think the bull is sick, Pa."

"What makes you think that?" Jacob asked. "Is it bad enough to get the doctor out here? We don't need to be finding ourselves another bull."

"I think I should just watch him."

"All right then. You do what you feel is right." Jacob glanced over at Melody. "Who cooked tonight?"

"Fiona. But tomorrow even she has admitted I can start doing what needs to be done for my family." Melody smiled, thrilled she wouldn't have to be treated like an invalid much longer.

"Well, good. I think you'll be much happier if you can move around and do what needs to be done instead of sitting in a chair reading to other people who are doing your chores."

"I will be much happier." Melody watched as Bastian got his food. "Did you have a good day at work?"

Bastian shrugged. "I got to work with the cattle, and I like to work with cattle. It makes me happy."

"Good."

"Do you think you're up for a short walk this evening?" Jacob asked Melody.

"I do. I'm really feeling almost completely better."

"Can you wear shoes?"

She frowned, thinking about it. "I think I could. Maybe I'll just wear some slippers though. Then they won't rub my feet so badly."

"Good idea," he said.

After she'd finished the dishes, they started out on their walk, and he led her straight to the house he was working on. The family called it the big house, so she was inclined to do the same.

"Your house is beautiful."

Jacob smiled. "My Henri helped me with it. She designed the whole kitchen with a cook in mind."

As he led her inside, she noted that the house was finished inside, but there was no furniture and the walls were yet to be painted. When he showed her the kitchen she gasped with delight. "Oh, Jacob. Cooking will be delightful in here. There's a real picture window to look out as I wash dishes. And a real stove." Without thinking, she threw her arms around him, thrilled that she was getting exactly what she wanted. He may not have built it for her, but it would be hers anyway.

"I take it you're happy with it?"

"Oh, yes. I want to plant flowers on either side of the front door, and I want to spend long winter nights here in front of the fireplace. Would it be all right if I invited the whole family for supper right after we move in? There's enough room for everyone here. This house is so big!"

She followed him up the stairs to see the three bedrooms there. "Why three?" she asked. Obviously, he wasn't planning to have more children.

He shrugged. "I thought it would be nice for the grandchildren to come visit and have a place to stay."

"You're really looking forward to those grandbabies, aren't you?"

He grinned. "I am. I can't tell you how much. Henri is going to make a good little mother."

"I'm sure all the girls will. It's been fun getting to know them. They make chores enjoyable."

"I'm glad. They're all good girls."

"Will this room be ours?" she asked, indicating the largest room there.

He nodded. "I figure I'll have our local furniture maker make us a huge bed. Then the grandkids can climb in bed with us in the mornings if they want to."

"I like that idea." Melody couldn't wait for grandbabies either.

When they got back to the house, he kept her hand in his, pulling her to the bedroom door. When he started kissing her and stroking her, she had no illusion about where their relationship was going. Right into that bed, apparently.

Within minutes, she was completely undressed, and she moved to the bed, spreading her legs slightly, waiting for him to fall on her and get it all over with. When he joined her in the middle of the bed, stroking her and his mouth began roaming over her entire body, she gave herself up to the feelings.

When he joined himself to her, there was only pleasure, which surprised her. It had always been slightly uncomfortable with Gideon. With Jacob there was nothing but pleasure.

That night she fell asleep with a smile on her lips. Her joy stronger than anything.

JACOB WAS ALREADY OUT doing his chores when she woke the next morning. She dressed carefully, in one of her two day dresses. She put her hair up in a stylish twist instead of her usual bun. She wanted to look nice for her new husband. It was a desire she hadn't had in a very long time.

While she cooked, she hummed to herself, thinking about the huge kitchen that would soon be at her disposal. The idea of living in that beautiful new house, and if she was honest with herself the enjoyable lovemaking from the night before, had put a new spring in her step.

Breakfast was on the table before the men came back in from their chores. She didn't know what her day would hold, but she was certain to be doing something with the girls.

After breakfast, the kiss Jacob gave her was anything but chaste. He was obviously trying to make up for lost time, and she couldn't blame him. The kissing and holding was wondrous and new. Jacob was just the man to wake her from what felt like a forty-year sleep.

When the girls arrived a short while later, Melody told them she wanted to get all non-essentials into crates before the move. "Would you mind helping me? I promise, I'm going to reciprocate."

"No need," Fiona said softly, looking at Henri. "Get to reading! We need to know what happens."

As the day went on, they learned more and more about Heathcliff and Catherine's volatile relationship while they packed away winter clothes and books, and so many other things.

"For a man who must have gotten rid of most of his things before starting on the trail, Jacob certainly does have a lot of things." Melody shook her head.

Fiona found a box with newsprint wrapping many small things. When they were unwrapped, Melody knew she'd found the collection of woodland animals Jacob had spoken of.

She unwrapped a few and was surprised to see how detailed they were. There was a rabbit, a deer, and so many others. Her favorite was a little bear cub looking up at his mother. It brought tears to her eyes it was so beautiful.

Jacob came home just before lunchtime to find the girls listening to Henri read while they packed things. "I just wanted to let you all know that we'll have furniture delivered tomorrow, so we should plan to move then."

Melody smiled. "That's wonderful. Thank you, Jacob." The way she said his name was almost a caress. She had never wanted to be physical with Gideon, but at that moment, if the girls hadn't been there, she would have taken Jacob by the arm and pulled him into their bedroom.

By the end of the day, everything they felt they could pack away had been done, and Melody had to keep herself from carrying things over to the big house. She'd never seen such a grand home, and oh how she wanted to live there. The idea of waiting even one more day seemed like pure torture.

When the girls left for the day, they agreed to meet back at the big house the following morning to help unpack. The men were to be there bright and early to move their belongings. Melody was thankful she only had the one trunk to deal with.

They had shepherd's pie for supper, something her aunt had taught her to make during the year she lived with her. It had become her favorite meal, and she was happy to share it with Jacob and Bastian.

After supper, Jacob took her for a short walk down to the creek to show her where their water had come from most days. "We just finished digging a well, though, and you'll be able to get water from that a lot easier than you can get it from the creek."

She was huffing and puffing as they came back up the hill. "It's hard to believe I made it up Big Hill just days ago, isn't it?"

He laughed. "I think you're in fine shape," he said.

She smiled at him, not even a little shy with the man after their night together. "Well, I'm glad you think so."

"Tomorrow is going to be a long day, but I think you ladies will enjoy unpacking and setting things about. We painted the walls today, and that was the last thing we needed to do before the furniture arrived. I hope you'll like what I've chosen."

"Oh, I'm certain I will. You don't mind if I make curtains and a tablecloth?"

"Not at all. You girls should feel free to decorate while we men work. I'm glad Henri is spending all her time with you. Then we know if she's in labor someone can fetch Mrs. Mitchell."

"Will she not have the doctor with her?" Melody asked.

"The doctor will be standing by, ready to come up the hill if needed. Roy is to get Mrs. Mitchell and stop at the doctor's on the way to let him know there's about to be a birth. We really like the doctor a great deal."

"Oh, that's good. I suppose you have everything ready then. One of us can go straight down to get Roy as soon as she's in labor." Melody felt safe with the plans they'd made. The baby was to be her grandchild after all.

Chapter Seven

Move day took everything Melody had in her. It wasn't her feet, but it was deciding where to put everything. Even with the girls, there was a lot of work to be done.

When they finished the big house, Melody and the girls went back to the cabin to clean where furniture had been before, and to move all of Bastian's belongings into the bedroom from the loft.

Henri read to them the whole while, but it was obvious to Melody that she was itching to get up and help.

It was shortly before suppertime when the girls left, and Melody went to the big house alone for the first time. She looked around her beautiful new kitchen, thinking she wanted curtains in a sunny yellow. Then she found the food they'd brought over from the cabin and she made a meal.

There was no fresh bread, which she hated, but she was still able to cook a meal she knew Jacob and Bastian would like. She had no idea whether Bastian planned to eat with them that night, but she would make enough for him to join if he wanted to.

The following day, they were going to work on the garden and harvest all they could. Melody looked forward to getting her hands dirty as she dug for potatoes and pulled carrots. She truly loved to garden more than anything else.

When Jacob came into the house at the end of the day, he was alone. "Is Bastian coming?" Melody asked.

"Bastian decided to have supper with Emma and Jared. He said he's going to spread the Bastian around."

Melody laughed. "I think he'll be much happier spending time with people his own age than us."

Jacob walked to her and wrapped his arms around her. "And to be honest, I'm happy to spend my time alone with you."

She rested her head on his shoulder and sighed contentedly. She may not love this man yet, but she felt it coming. He'd turned her life around and she was incredibly grateful to have found him.

After supper, they sat together with her working on the hat and booties for the baby, and him working on his woodland critter. "Do you know what you're making yet?"

He shook his head. "No, it hasn't told me."

"I found your box of animals yesterday. Would you mind if I displayed them? I won't if it would bother you."

A slight smile crossed his face. "If you like them, then I think they should be displayed. If you don't, then we'll just keep them in the box."

"Oh, I absolutely adore them. Thank you."

Jacob felt both happy and sad that she loved the animals he'd made for his first wife. It was getting harder and harder to think about his children's mother as he spent time with Melody.

"You've done a good job with the house," he said. "Are you planning to do anything else?"

She laughed. "As soon as I finish this project, I plan to make curtains for the kitchen and a tablecloth to match. Then I'll make curtains for the dining room and parlor. This house is so grand, it's going to take me a year to get all that I want to do done for it. I also want to make quilts for each bed. It's a good thing the girls were part of the package when I married you."

"I'm glad you get along with them all so well. Henri has missed having her mother around so much, but she seems more content now that you're here. I know she hates that she couldn't share her baby with her mother."

Melody frowned. "I know I can't be a mother to her, but I will be a good grandmother to her children." She looked out the window and saw that it was already dark. "I think I'm going to go get ready for bed."

He grinned. "I'll be there in a few minutes."

THE DAY IN THE GARDEN was just what Melody needed. She sat right on the ground and used a spade to dig up potatoes. Henri refused to be excluded from the harvest. She'd helped with the planting and some of the weeding. She wouldn't miss out on harvesting the crops they'd so carefully cultivated.

"Are we going to put up whatever we harvest today in the next day or two?" Melody asked, thinking what a huge job it would be. There were so many different vegetables in the garden, she had no doubt it would be a good winter for them.

"Yes," Fiona said. "We'll split between families evenly with anything left over going to the pastor and his wife. Hannah's been too busy with that new baby of hers to get any real gardening done."

"I can understand that," Melody said. "It's the community's job to care for the pastor and his wife anyway."

Emma nodded. "I'm excited that we have such a fine bounty. It's going to be fun to look out for others this year!"

"What do you mean?" Melody asked.

"During the winter months, we will visit with the elderly and take them a cake or a pie. Or we'll make meals for those we know are facing hardship. Or just go over and watch someone's children so she can get some chores done. Pastor Jed started it last fall when we were all trying to settle in and scared about whether we'd have enough food for the winter to come."

"That's really nice. I want to be part of it!"

"Oh, good! The new schoolteacher is my first project," Emma said. "The men built her a teacherage as soon as she said she'd stay, but she has no family left. She lost both of her parents over the winter. I think she's going to need some company at times."

"That makes sense. Maybe we have her over for lunch every Saturday, and we can all eat in my new dining room. That would make me so happy!" Melody looked forward to entertaining in her beautiful new home.

"That could be a lot of fun," Fiona grinned. "I'm glad I don't have to try to find friends. I have three of my favorite people to spend time with every day."

While Fiona and Melody were fixing a cold lunch for them to eat outside, Emma came barreling into Fiona's cabin. "Go get Mrs. Mitchell! The baby's coming!"

Fiona didn't need to be asked twice. She dropped the tomato she was cutting up for their sandwiches and ran to hitch up the wagon.

Melody finished fixing lunch for them all. First babies were never quick to make an appearance. She carried their lunch to the cabin, meeting Mrs. Mitchell on the way in. "I helped birth a lot of babies on the trail, but I'm not a midwife."

Mrs. Mitchell nodded. "If you want to help, I'd be happy to have another set of hands."

The labor took hours. Emma left to make a meal for the men but returned immediately. Mrs. Mitchell was a no-nonsense woman who took charge of the situation, barking out orders to anyone there.

Just after midnight that night, Melody helped ease her first grandbaby into the world, determined to love her with all her heart. She washed the baby while Mrs. Mitchell tended to Henri.

It was a little girl, and Melody's heart was immediately stolen. This was a child who she would have a real connection with. A child who would always be in her life. What more could a woman ask for?

The baby was named Nellie Norma after the women who had given her parents' life.

When she stepped outside, she could see the men gathered around. "Let's go home, Grandpa," Melody said to Jacob. She would wait until they were out of earshot to tell him he had a granddaughter. One she would share with him.

THEY FINISHED THE HARVEST without Henri, using Melody's kitchen to put up the vegetables. Each day one of them would sit with Henri, helping her with the baby and other chores until she was ready to do it all on her own.

Melody loved her time with Henri and little Nellie. The baby was a joy to be around, and Melody tried to memorize each minute they had together while she was this small.

"Can I get you anything?" she asked, while Henri fed her daughter.

"Maybe some milk. I'm afraid I won't make enough. She seems to always be hungry." Henri stared lovingly into her daughter's eyes while nursing her.

"I'll get the milk. Do you want lunch soon?"

"I would. Thank you, Melody. You've been a real blessing."

"I'm certain your mother-in-law would be here if I wasn't. She loves that baby as much as we do."

Henri smiled. "I was a little nervous when Pa first married you. I wasn't sure that you were going to be the kind of woman who would open her heart to your husband's children. I was wrong to be nervous though. I feel like if my ma were here, she'd give her blessing to your marriage with Pa. You make him happy, and that's plain for all to see."

"Thank you," Melody said with tears in her eyes. "I already love you. And this entire family. I wasn't sure if it would come naturally, but it has. What a wonderful family for me to marry into."

"I like that. I think it's time for me to be on my own with the baby after today, though. You and the others have devoted all your time to helping me, and the harvest needs to be put up. And the men need to start hunting soon. I feel well enough to take care of Nellie and cook meals now."

"Are you sure?" Melody asked.

Henri nodded, smiling sweetly. "I'm sure. I won't be as much help as I could be this year, so I can't keep you from helping."

"All right. But if you realize you're doing too much too soon, I want you to let me know. We're handling the harvest well."

"Just think. In another month we'll have all the food we need for the winter. Pa said he's going to butcher a few steers, so we'll even have beef through the winter. I think we're going to thrive here."

"And I will as well." Melody fixed them a light lunch, and once the baby was asleep, they ate it at the table together. "I have loved every minute of taking care of you and Nellie. Thank you for letting me be part of it."

"I couldn't have done it without you."

MELODY AND THE GIRLS finished getting the entire harvest put up the day before the first snow of the year. "This snow is so early!" she said.

The other two shook their heads. "We get a lot of snow here. Don't worry though. Pa made a sleigh we all share through the winter," Emma told her. "It's so much fun gliding over the snow that way."

"Will the men still be able to get the meat we need?" Melody asked, worried about the winter.

"Oh, yes!" Fiona told her. "We don't have to hurry quite so much with putting up the meat when it's already frozen outside."

"All right. Bring on the snow then!"

Emma grinned. "My brother Roy is the best hunter of all of us. Soon, he'll just start showing up at random times with a buck or a rabbit. He usually goes for large game. Last year we ended up with more than we needed for the winter."

"I'm not going to worry then."

"Don't!" Emma said. "Besides, Pa said he'd butcher a few steers as well. We are going to be more than ready for winter."

"Oh, I have so many inside projects I want to do this winter. But I'll certainly miss spending so much time with you girls?"

"Why?" Fiona asked. "We'll keep spending time together. Emma and I can walk here easily, and Roy will bring Henri and the baby up the hill. You probably need to get a cradle for her though."

"I'll talk to Jacob about it. Oh, I'm glad we're going to include each other in our winter plans."

"Me too!" Emma said. "I think I'd feel very lonely without my family at my side."

"Do your mother or sisters ever join you?" Melody asked. She'd felt badly for not inviting Emma's sisters and mother to join them.

"They did all the time last year," Emma said. "Then the girls started school, and Ma said she was enjoying her time alone too much to keep joining us."

Melody smiled. After so many years of being alone, she was happy to have other women nearby. The work was so much easier with good company.

"I'm going to talk to Jacob about making one of the rooms upstairs into a nursery. Then we can be certain Nellie will have a place to sleep here. It feels strange not including Henri in all we're doing right now, but I do agree that she should stay home and get used to the duties of being a mother."

"Henri really does need the time alone with the baby," Emma said. "Ma told me every time she had a baby, she'd send her older children to stay with Pa's parents because she needed that time alone with each of us to fall in love with her babies. Ma's a terrible cook, but she's a good mother."

"Is her cooking really that bad?" Melody asked. She'd heard several people say how bad it was now.

"Yes!" Emma and Fiona said together.

"Now I want to go to her house for a meal, just to try her cooking."

Emma laughed. "Oh, it wouldn't work. Ma has a deal with Henri and me. If she invites people over, one of us will cook for them. She doesn't think she should have to go through the embarrassment of people knowing she can't cook worth a lick. Her sewing is amazing though. She taught all three of us girls to love to sew. I'm almost done with a little gown I made for the baby," Emma said. "I'm knitting lace for the collar and cuffs on the sleeves. It will be nice to have Nellie looking so pretty for church on Sundays."

"Nellie would look beautiful if she went naked to church on Sundays," Melody said.

They all laughed. "That would certainly be messy," Fiona said.

"I'm sure even Pastor Jed, who doesn't get ruffled by many things, wouldn't think a naked baby in church is a good idea," Emma said, grinning.

Melody removed the jars in the canning pot and set them on the worktable. "That's the last of it. We have no more vegetables to put up."

"We'll have to tell the men it's time to go hunting then," Emma said. "Good job, ladies."

Chapter Eight

October was a month of preparing for winter. The men all took turns hunting, and came back with whatever they'd killed for the women to deal with. Toward the end of the month, to her surprise, Melody could no longer cut the meat off the carcasses. She vomited each time she tried, and finally went to sit in the kitchen. All her life she'd dealt with fresh meat, and not being able to was very strange for her. It was like her entire body had changed overnight.

Fiona worried the most about her. She sat with her at the table after the third time she lost her lunch to talk to her about what was wrong. "Perhaps you have a stomach flu."

Melody shook her head. "No, I feel fine most of the time. It's just when I have to touch the bloody meat..." Melody got up and ran for a place to vomit. Just thinking about it was turning her stomach now.

"I'm taking you to the doctor," Fiona said once she was back. "There is something wrong, and we need to get to the bottom of it."

"We can't take time in the middle of butchering an elk to go to the doctor."

"Oh, yes we can. Emma, if you need help, get your mother or your sisters. We'll be back as soon as we can." With that, Fiona left the house and went to hitch up the wagon.

There were only a few inches of snow on the ground, but it was cold enough Melody had no desire to be out in the weather. She had to be when they were working on the meat, but it was only for a minute or two at a time, and the house was toasty warm.

On the drive, Fiona kept glancing at Melody to make sure she wasn't falling out of the wagon. "You're pale. I just know there's something wrong."

Thirty minutes later, Melody walked out of the doctor's house. She was shocked at what she'd heard the doctor say. She'd even argued with him until she was blue in the face.

He said she was pregnant, but she knew she was barren. She climbed into the wagon beside Fiona, who was watching her carefully. "Oh, he said it's something bad, didn't he?"

Melody shook her head. She wouldn't tell a soul before she told Jacob. He had four grown children and a grandchild, and he was going to have a fifth child. What man would want a baby in those circumstances?

"You're starting to really scare me, Melody. We all love you, and I'd hate to see something happen to you."

Melody's mind was dwelling on what to tell Jacob, and she didn't think she should tell the girl. "Tomorrow. We'll all talk tomorrow."

Through her shock, Melody noted the beautiful color of fall in Bear Lake. The trees were all changing colors, and she would soon change too. She would get round as fall and winter passed, most likely giving birth in late summer. Her life would be so different with an infant.

It wasn't simply that she thought she was barren, she'd believed she was too old to have a baby. And here she was, learning that she was expecting for the first time in her life.

Most of the work on the elk was done by the time they walked in the door. "The doctor doesn't want me dealing with the fresh meat any longer. I can do other parts of the processing, but I can't cut the meat off the carcasses. He said it was a very bad idea to keep doing so." Melody told the others the truth as far as it went.

How on earth was she supposed to tell Jacob?

When they were finished for the day, the girls helped her clean the kitchen and left, promising to be back the following day. While she made supper, she thought about what it would be like to have a baby of her own.

She could hold and nurse the baby, and never have to give it back. The idea of a child that would forever be hers, well, it seemed as wonderful as it did crazy.

She fixed a special meal that night. Jacob had butchered a hog, so she made pork chops with fried potatoes and carrots on the side. She hoped Jacob would be pleased with the meal, so she could find a way to tell him they were going to have a baby.

Jacob came inside to kiss her cheek. "Supper smells amazing," he said.

She smiled. "I hope it tastes as good as it smells."

"How was your day?" he asked.

She thought about telling him then. She really did. But instead she said, "Oh, we got the elk taken care of. There will be plenty of meat for the winter."

"Glad to hear it."

She put their supper on the table and added an extra plate to the table when Bastian walked in. So much for telling Jacob during supper.

Bastian talked animatedly through the whole meal. "I'm glad I was wrong about the bull being sick. We need to make sure to keep him out of the pasture with the cows though because they are all already calving. And that bull doesn't seem to know when to quit." He shook his head, continuing his talk about the bull.

Melody was mostly quiet, still wondering how to tell Jacob she was expecting. Watching him with Bastian, she was certain he loved his children more than anything. But did he love them enough that he wanted more at his age? That's the only thing she was unsure about.

After supper, Bastian stayed and talked to Jacob while she did the dishes, and she washed as slowly as she could, waiting for him to be done.

Once all the dishes were wiped and put up, and her kitchen was in its usual pristine condition, she went up the stairs to get ready for bed.

Normally she enjoyed Bastian's visits, but there was just too much on her mind for her to listen to him talk as much as he was.

She slipped into bed, not certain she'd be able to sleep, but not wanting to stay awake anymore either. She was actually scared of her sweet, gentle husband, and how he would react to her news, which was silly because he'd never even given her a look that would frighten her. He was a good man.

When Jacob joined her a short while later, he pulled her close. "Is everything all right? You were very quiet tonight."

"I have something I need to tell you, and I don't want you to get angry about it."

"Why would I get angry? Were you making eyes at some other man or something?"

"Nothing like that, but I did see a man today. Dr. Bentley."

Jacob was surprised. "The doctor? Are you sick?"

"No, I thought I was sick, but instead, I'm expecting."

Jacob said nothing for a full minute. "You said you were barren."

"I thought I was." She said a silent prayer that he wouldn't be angry.

"Melody, I've raised my children. They're all grown. I'm a grandfather!"

"I know." Melody felt tears drifting down her cheeks. "I didn't think this could happen, but now that it has, I can't be upset. I've wanted a baby for so long! I thought I was barren. I thought I was too old to have a baby. I was ready to be content to be a grandmother, but it didn't work out that way. We'll have a baby in the summer."

Jacob rolled away from her onto his back, staring up at the ceiling. "I'm not sure I want to be a father again."

"I understand." But she didn't. To her, finding out she was expecting the child she never thought she could have was a wondrous thing. She would love the child within her with all her heart and all her soul. She loved Jacob as well, though she hadn't realized it until that moment.

It was a long while before either of them fell asleep. She understood why he didn't necessarily want a baby at his age, but she wasn't sure he understood why it was what she wanted with everything inside her.

The following morning was no better. Jacob had little to say to her, and she hoped he would slowly come to understand how she felt and warm up to the idea of having another child. If he didn't, she had no idea what she'd do. Divorce wasn't something she could even think about.

After he'd left for the day without the kiss he usually bestowed on her cheek, she washed the dishes, but she didn't look out to see the beauty that was the valley she lived in. Instead, she did her chores, and felt numb inside. The man she loved didn't want the child she carried.

When Fiona and Emma arrived, they had Henri and the baby with them. The girls all delighted over the baby and how red her cheeks were from the cold. Melody tried not to look at the child, because it would just make her yearn for her child and her husband's love.

After a short while, Melody realized everyone was looking at her. She was normally right there wherever the baby was.

"What did the doctor say?" Fiona asked. "You said you'd tell me today."

Melody took a deep breath and the tears started. In less than a minute she was sobbing, not sure what she was supposed to do, and not sure if she should tell the others. Not until Jacob made peace with the situation.

Emma hurried to her and hugged her close. "Oh, it can't be that bad!"

"It's the best news I've ever gotten in my life," Melody choked out between sobs. "I'm expecting, and we always thought I was barren."

Fiona squealed with excitement and hugged her tightly. Emma smiled and patted her happily. Only Henri seemed to understand. "You're going to have a child, my brother or sister, who will be younger than my baby?"

Melody nodded, plopping herself down at the table across from Henri. "I've wanted a baby for so long, but your pa...well, he's made it clear that he's already raised his children. He doesn't want more, but I desperately want this baby. He's barely spoken to me since I told him."

Finally understanding, Emma and Fiona joined them at the table. "He doesn't want it?" Emma asked. "But he's such a good father."

"He's a lot older now," Henri said. "He thought he was done raising children."

Melody nodded, getting her sobs under control. It seemed that everyone was starting to understand. "I don't know if he's going to ever be all right with the baby, and I don't think I could ever be all right without it."

"That's a fine pickle you're in," Emma said, sighing loudly. "Did he forget how babies were made? I know you didn't just get pregnant on your own!"

Fiona started giggling at that. "I'm sorry. He just has four children. He knows how they're made!"

When the others didn't share her mirth, Fiona stopped. "We're here for you always. I'm sure if it comes to that, Bastian would move in with Pa, and you could move into the cabin."

"Maybe," Melody said. But the truth was, she didn't want to live apart from Jacob. She loved him, and she enjoyed every minute of their time together. He was very good to her.

The door opened, and Jared was there. "I just shot a buck." He looked between the women, confused, but he didn't say anything.

"We'll take care of it," Emma called.

Melody hoped he didn't tell his father she'd been crying. That was the last thing she wanted Jacob to know.

"So you can't cut the meat," Henri said. "Why don't you sit with the baby, and I'll do your share of the preserving?"

"Oh, you don't have to do that!" Melody said.

"Oh, but I want to. Besides, you need the practice."

Melody realized that Henri had yet to say anything about the pregnancy, but she was obviously going to support her through it. That was really all Melody needed. Someone to lean on through the next eight months.

She looked down into Nellie's sleeping face, and she knew that no matter what it took. She wanted the child she carried, and no one would be able to convince her it was a bad idea. Why, God had provided a miracle, and if Jacob couldn't see that, then perhaps he wasn't a man of God as he said.

She refused to do penance for something that had been out of her control, and she looked forward to every moment of raising her child.

Each of the girls hugged her as they left at the end of the day, showing silent support of the situation she found herself in. Melody stood tall, hugging them each and thanking them for being on her side.

While she made supper—a roast from one of the butchered steers—she decided she wouldn't be quiet about it. She would talk to him about the baby and about turning one of the upstairs bedrooms into a nursery. She was going to enjoy every minute of expecting the child within her. No matter what Jacob said or did.

Jacob walked into the house at the end of the day, worried that he had no words to say. He didn't have a right to be angry with her because he'd had as much a part in making the baby as she did.

He didn't greet her with the usual kiss, instead going into the kitchen and calmly washing his hands. "You feeling all right?"

Melody nodded. "I really only get sick when I touch the meat with blood dripping off it, so I'm watching the baby while the girls put up the meat."

He remembered how hard the first few months had always been on Nellie, and he started to say something, but he didn't know what to say. He'd just married her, and just realized he loved her, and she was already expecting. It was too soon. Much too soon.

Melody pretended he was acting normally, and she set the table for them. "Do you know if Bastian is coming tonight?"

Jacob shook his head. "No, he's going to eat with Sam and Fiona. He said that Fiona makes the best beef pot pies in the whole world."

"Do you like pot pies as much as Bastian does?" she asked.

"They've always been a favorite. Nellie made them at least once a week. Sometimes chicken, sometimes beef, always delicious."

"I'll get Fiona's receipt then. I'll happily make you pot pies." Anything to keep him happy while he was grappling with the idea of their baby.

Chapter Nine

The winter was just as cold as they thought it would be, but all their preparations paid off. By late spring, Melody was as big as a house. She and Jacob were getting along well again, but he had never expressed any excitement over the baby.

When it was time to plant their garden, the girls told her to sit and watch, taking care of the baby, who was crawling everywhere.

Melody shook her head. "No, I love to play with the baby, as you all know, but I want to spend some time digging in the dirt. It's cathartic."

So they all watched the baby while they planted their garden. "We need to plant some raspberry bushes," Melody said as she looked around. "They'd give us raspberries every year. I have a receipt for the most delicious raspberry muffins."

"Wait 'til you taste huckleberries," Henri said. "They grow in the mountains around here, so we'll take a day, go up into the forest at the top of those mountains over there, and we'll spend the whole afternoon picking huckleberries."

"I'm not sure how many mountains I'm going to be climbing this summer!" Melody said, patting her huge belly.

"I won't be able to climb either. Not this summer." Fiona said.

"Are you expecting as well?" Emma asked. At Fiona's nod, she continued. "Why didn't you tell us?"

Fiona shrugged. "I just found out a couple of weeks ago. Sam and I have been enjoying our little secret, but since I'll be showing before too long…"

"Well, I hope all these babies become good friends," Melody said with a smile. "Their aunt or uncle will need friends."

"Are you still doing well?" Emma asked.

Melody nodded. "I am. The doctor is seeing me more than he usually would because of my age, but as far as he can tell the baby is fine."

Henri smiled at that. "Good. It'll be nice not to be the youngest anymore. How's Pa acting about it?"

Melody shrugged. "He's still not exactly happy about the baby, but he doesn't seem angry about it either."

Melody climbed to her feet after finishing an entire row of carrots, looking at herself and laughing. "I think I'm wearing enough dirt for now." She walked toward the quilt where the baby was sleeping. They'd discovered putting her on a quilt was magic. She didn't like how the grass felt, so she didn't leave the quilt.

As she was walking, she tripped over a clump of dirt, gasping as she fell, turning herself so her belly wouldn't take the brunt of her weight. "That hurt."

The others surrounded her. "Are you all right?" Emma asked.

"I think so. I just tripped."

"I'll run and get Pa," Henri said.

"Don't bother him. I'm fine." Melody sat up with the help of Emma and Fiona, gasping in pain. "My ankle."

Fiona looked at her ankle while Henri ran for Jacob. She obviously didn't believe Melody was all right.

Fiona frowned at what she saw. Melody's right foot was twisted sideways. "Stay with her," Fiona told Emma. "I'm going to hitch up the wagon. She needs to go to the doctor. That ankle is broken."

"It might be better to have the doctor come here," Emma said.

"Either way, I need to hitch up the wagon."

Emma frowned at Melody. "Why did you do that? Now you won't be able to help us in the garden!"

Melody sighed. "I assure you, it wasn't intentional. It's bad enough being pregnant all summer. Now I won't be able to walk to feel the cool breeze."

"I hope you didn't hurt the baby," Emma said softly.

"Oh, I really don't think I did. Otherwise, I'd be rolling down that hill to get to the doctor. We wouldn't be waiting for Jacob or a wagon."

Melody felt foolish sitting on the ground, covered in dirt. "Help me to the house. I don't want to go to the doctor with this much dirt all over me."

Emma shook her head. "I will not. You're staying right there at least until Pa gets here."

Jacob came running around the corner of the house. "Are you hurt? Will you be okay? Did you hurt the baby?"

"I'm hurt. I think my ankle is broken. I don't think I hurt the baby. The girls are insisting I see the doctor."

Jacob nodded, worry covering his face. "I will drive you." He scooped her up into his arms as if he was a man half his age, carrying her to the wagon, which Fiona had finished hitching.

He set her carefully on the seat before climbing up himself and taking the leads. "Would you like me to come?" Fiona asked.

Jacob didn't bother to respond as he began the drive down the hill to the doctor. "How did you do this?" he finally asked, watching her face as she flinched in pain.

She knew he was trying to distract her, but she desperately needed to be distracted. "I was helping in the garden, and when I stood up to go sit with Nellie on the quilt, I tripped over a clump of dirt and fell. I made sure to land on my side and not on my belly."

"I'm much more worried about you than I am the baby." Deep in his heart, he wasn't sure if that was true. He loved Melody, but he wouldn't be able to bear it if she had to go through the sadness of losing her baby. He knew it would tear her apart.

At the doctor's house, he carried her to the door, and knocked loudly. Dr. Bentley opened the door, saw them, and opened it wide so Jacob could carry his wife inside. "She fell and her ankle appears to be broken."

"Put her on the table," the doctor said, indicating his examination table. "I'll check her ankle, but I also need to be sure she didn't harm herself or the baby in any other way. Do you want to wait in the parlor?" The doctor's house doubled as his office.

"No, I want to be here with my wife."

When it was time to set Melody's ankle, Jacob held her under her shoulders while the doctor pulled. Her whimper made him feel like the worst man alive. He never would have allowed Nellie to garden while she was expecting. Why hadn't he been more careful with Melody?

"Your ankle should be healed by the time the baby is born. I hope you'll have help until then."

"Yes, my daughters will all help."

Melody loved the way he included his daughters-in-law in with his daughter, as if there was no distinction between them. Melody nodded. "They are wonderful."

"Good. Now, if you'll step out of the room, Jacob, I need to do a personal exam."

"She is carrying my baby, doctor. I think it will be just fine if I see her unclothed."

Melody hid a smile. It was really the first time Jacob had referred to the baby as his own. It was definitely a step in the right direction.

While the doctor did the exam, Jacob held her hand, trying to assure her. "The baby will be fine. They are strong."

The doctor finished his exam and smiled. "Jacob is right. You are doing fine. Jacob, you should make her two crutches, so she can get around some. We want her to be strong enough to give birth in a couple of months, so she needs to be able to move around some. I would make sure she had a bed on the first floor, even if you have to turn your dining room into a bedroom."

Jacob nodded. "I will make the crutches tonight."

"Good. No weight on that ankle. If you have any spotting, I want you to come to me right away, but I think you and the baby will be just fine."

"Thank you," Melody said, relieved that the baby would be all right.

Instead of taking her directly home, Jacob took her to Fiona's cabin and deposited her on the bed. "Once we turn our house upside down, I will come back for you."

Fiona and Emma both hurried into the cabin to check on her. "What did the doctor say?"

"I didn't hurt the baby, but I did break my ankle. I'm going to need help again."

"Of course, you will!" Emma said. "We've already been talking about it. Did the doctor say you needed to stay in bed, or can you sit up?"

"He wants me to do whatever I can do without putting weight on my ankle. The men are at our house turning my dining room into a bedroom for me." Melody shook her head. "He listened to every word the doctor said, and I have a feeling he won't let me do one thing differently."

"And he's sure the baby is all right?" Emma asked.

"He said to watch for spotting and to see him immediately if that happens, but he thinks I'll be fine." Melody said a silent prayer of thanks that her baby was going to be fine. After so long, there was no way she could lose that baby.

When Jacob came for her, Jared offered to carry her, and Jacob glared at his oldest son. "She's my wife, and I will carry her."

He picked her up, carrying her to the big house and into the dining room where their bed had been put. They would have had to take it apart and reassemble it, but he obviously didn't care. In that moment, she felt more cherished than she had in a long time.

While she lay in the bed, Jacob moved a small table to her side of the bed. "You can put drinks there. You will stay in the bed unless I get you out of it. Do you understand?"

Melody nodded. "I'll do my best."

He narrowed his eyes. "You will simply do as you are told."

Finally, she nodded. Emma and Fiona had followed her there. "We're going to make supper and get you as comfortable as you can be."

Emma propped pillows behind her head so she could sit up, while Fiona started supper. "I guess I won't be able to help in the garden like I wanted," Melody said frowning. She was feeling just a little bit sorry for herself. "I won't even be able to go outside with you."

"Do you think Pa will carry you out to your rocking chair? Then you could at least watch us," Emma said. "Oh, we could finish *Wuthering Heights*!"

Melody laughed. "I may be able to do that in a few days. Doc wants me to have my foot propped all the time for the first three days."

"Then we'll open your window, and you can watch us and yell out what we're doing wrong!" Emma winked at Melody.

"I would never!"

"No, but you could read very loudly!" Fiona called from the kitchen.

"I could do that," Melody said, thankful the girls were trying to find ways to include her even after she'd hurt herself.

When supper was finished, Emma pulled a chair to Melody's bedside. "Fiona is going to cook supper and have Jared and I over, so I can stay with you until Jacob is back for the day."

"Thank you," Melody said softly. "The doctor gave me some medicine, and it's making me sleepy."

"Sleep then. I'll just sit here and read ahead on Wuthering Heights."

"You will not! All of us read it or none of us read it."

"That's a silly rule," Emma said.

"But it's one we made together the day we started the book."

Emma sighed. "All right. I won't read it. Here, I'll sing you a lullaby." As soon as Emma started singing, Melody wanted to beg her to read the book instead, but they'd all agreed, and she could handle Emma's singing. If she had to...

When Melody woke a while later, Jacob was home. He brought her supper, and ate his own sitting in the bed alongside her. "You can eat at the kitchen table if you want," Melody said.

"I could, but I'd rather sit here with you."

"Tell me what you did today, then. You already know what I did."

"I do. There were several calves birthed this morning. Only one needed help. Bastian hurried around like a proud father, talking to each of the cows. It's funny just how connected to them he feels."

Melody could picture Bastian doing just that. It made her smile just to think about. "That sounds like Bastian."

"Two of the hogs had piglets today. The day was all about birthing I guess I should say."

"It sounds like it. How many piglets?"

"Eighteen total. We'll sell a couple of the males in the fall and butcher a few more. I think we'll have enough meat that we can sell some of it."

Melody smiled, shaking her head. "You certainly have a talent for making money."

Jacob grinned. "Always have. When other boys were playing games, I was asking all the people in town if I could do odd jobs. I saved every penny I made too. I was a farmer back east, but I always wanted to own a huge ranching operation. The prices were just too high, so I decided to come west with my boys."

"You certainly have a huge ranch here. I like that you work with your boys the way you do. I'm sure they enjoy it as well. Do you think you'll need to take on ranch hands anytime soon?"

"I do. I think we'll need to do it by roundup. We have just too many calves to work on our own this year. I'm really looking forward to finding some help. We'll be selling a few of the calves to anyone who wants them. The rest we'll either add to the herd or fatten up to sell in the fall. We'll have to drive the cattle to market this year. I'll send the boys though. I wouldn't want to be gone when the baby is born."

"The baby is going to be here in July," she said, smiling slightly. She couldn't believe he was unsure of her due date after all this time.

"Well, then I'll be here to help around the ranch. I've already told the boys two of them are going, and they can choose which two. Bastian will go because he has no family to leave behind. I'm not sure who it will be between Sam and Jared."

"Jared," Melody said with a smile. "Fiona is expecting."

"I didn't know that! How long have they known?"

"Fiona said they were keeping it to themselves for a few weeks, but she told us today. We'll have another grandbaby."

Jacob smiled. "Another grandchild to play with our child. Marrying you turned my whole world upside down."

Chapter Ten

During her convalescence, Jacob was at her side as often as possible. He let the boys do the majority of the work, while he took care of Melody.

At the beginning of July, he carried her up the stairs to show her something. One of the spare rooms had been converted into a nursery. There was a cradle she could tell he'd made himself. There was a small quilt hanging off one side of the cradle. "Who made this?" she asked, picking it up and holding it to her face, as she balanced on one foot.

"I paid one of the ladies in town to do it. I hope you like it."

"I love it all." She turned and threw her arms around him, laughing when they were still a full foot apart due to the baby she was carrying.

"I'm glad. I've been working on this surprise for a while."

"Thank you so much for thinking to do something so special." She could see a dresser there in the room. "What's in that?" she asked.

"Lots of diapers. Got some white cotton from the store and the girls cut it to make diapers. There are little gowns in there that different people in town sewed for a small fee. Should be everything we need for the baby. At least for a while."

"Oh, and one other thing that's not up here." He scooped her up and carried her down the stairs and to the front door. He set her down right outside the front door, and she looked around, spotting a baby carriage.

"Where did this come from? You didn't make it!"

He shook his head. "No, I had Herbert Jensen order it for me. It took a while to get here, but I thought you'd want to use it. I bought one for Henri while I was at it. With as often as all you girls are outside, it should be nice for both of you to have one. I didn't order one for

Fiona because I didn't know she was expecting when I ordered the other two."

"I'm sure I can share with her." Melody leaned against him, holding her hurt ankle in the air. "Thank you."

"You're very welcome. It's the least I could do after acting like a heel when you told me you were expecting. I should have apologized long ago, but I didn't think words could ever be enough." He took a deep breath. "I love my children with everything inside me, and I've been looking forward to grandchildren for years. I never expected to have any more children of my own though."

"Of course not. You're youngest is almost twenty now."

He nodded. "But even though I didn't expect to have more, it doesn't make our baby any less important. You've never had a child, and every woman deserves children. I know you were accepting mine as your own, and loving the grandbaby, but you spent your whole life thinking you couldn't have a baby, and when it happened for you, I should have treated it like the miracle it is. Not like it was something you did wrong." He scooped her up and carried her back inside, putting her in her favorite chair. "Will you forgive me?"

"I was never angry with you. I understood. I played through all the ways you could feel in my head before I told you about the baby. I was worried you wouldn't want me around anymore."

"Of course, I do. I love you." The words were simple, but they were exactly what she needed to hear.

"I love you too, Jacob."

He leaned down to kiss her. "I'm going to be awfully glad when you can walk again."

She laughed. "I will too. I'm so tired of being stuck wherever you put me. The crutches help, of course, but they hurt my arms. I worry that using them too much will hurt the baby, which doesn't make any sense at all, but it doesn't stop the worries."

He chuckled. "I'm glad you came along when you did. I can't imagine life without you anymore."

"You took me in when I was at the lowest point in my life, but that's not why I love you. I love you for how gentle and tender you are with me. For the special looks you share with each of your children. Or the joy on your face when you found out you had a granddaughter. There are so many things I love about you, I can't even count them all."

"I promise that I'm going to be just as devoted a father as I was with my first four. And if you get pregnant again, I'll know it's another miracle from God."

Finally, Melody felt content with the world.

Epilogue

Melody sat in her bed, which was still in the middle of the dining room for some reason, holding her newborn daughter. From the moment she'd learned she was expecting, she'd prayed the baby would be a girl. She'd have loved a boy just as much, but the idea of a girl caught hold of her, and she couldn't imagine anything else.

Jacob walked into the room, looking down at the child. "Doc wouldn't tell me if it was a boy or a girl."

"It's a girl. What should we call her?" She'd had dozens of names picked out, and she'd forgotten every one of them when she'd looked into her child's face.

"How would you feel about Angela? Because she's our little miracle. Our angel."

"I think that's perfect."

Jacob carefully sat on the bed beside her. "Are you feeling all right?"

Melody smiled, nodding. "Never in my life have I dreamed of having such a perfect moment. Sitting with the man I love, holding the child that I've always wanted. Thank you, Jacob, for giving me such a wonderful life."

"Thank you for my little girl."

www.ingramcontent.com/pod-product-compliance
Lightning Source LLC
Chambersburg PA
CBHW051254160726
47994CB00003B/1167